This book belongs to

_____

_____

_____

Age _____

Adapted from the originals by Anne McKie.
Illustrated by Ken McKie.

Published by
GRANDREAMS LIMITED
Jadwin House, 205/211 Kentish Town Road, London, NW5 2JU.

Printed in Czech Republic.

Fairy Tales in this book

Snow White

Pinocchio

The Three Bears

Beauty and The Beast

**plus a selection of your favourite
Nursery Rhymes**

SNOW WHITE

Once upon a time a lovely little Princess was born. She had hair as black as coal and skin as white as snow. "I know," smiled the Queen, as she gazed at her baby. "I shall call her Snow White!"

But soon after the little Princess was born, the Queen died, leaving the King very unhappy and lonely.

After some years had passed — and Snow White had grown up into a young lady — the King married again. His new Queen was very beautiful and also very vain.

On the wall of her room, the new Queen kept a magic mirror.

Because she couldn't bear to know of anyone more beautiful than herself, the Queen would look in her mirror every day and say, "Magic Mirror on the wall, who is the fairest one of all?" And the mirror would answer, "You are the fairest one of all!"

Now one dreadful day when the Queen asked her mirror the usual question, the mirror replied. "Snow White is the fairest one of all!"

The Queen was so angry and jealous she almost smashed the mirror.

As the Queen stood glowering into the mirror, she thought of a plan. She sent for her huntsman and ordered him to kill Snow White. The huntsman wished he had not been chosen to do such a dreadful thing, but he dare not disobey the wicked Queen.

He lifted Snow White onto his horse and rode with her deeper and deeper into the forest.

At last they stopped and Snow White begged him to spare her life.

The huntsman was far too kind to kill the beautiful Princess. Instead he rode quickly away — leaving Snow White in the care of the animals who roamed the forest.

Snow White spent all the day wandering through the trees. At first she felt frightened, but one by one the animals came out from their hiding places and made friends.

The time passed very quickly and soon it began
to get dark. Some of the birds and animals seemed
to be leading Snow White along a special path,
so she followed them.

The forest path led to the strangest little house
Snow White had ever seen. And finding no-one at
home, she opened the door and walked
right in.

Everything inside the house was very small. The ceiling was so low, that Snow White had to bend her head to walk about. "Whoever lives here must be very tiny!" laughed Snow White, as she picked up the dainty cups and bowls.

"There seems to be seven of everything," she gasped, as she looked round the room. "Seven chairs to sit on, seven pipes to smoke and seven pairs of slippers."

Now this was the home of the seven dwarfs who worked all day in the mountains digging for gold.

Snow White felt so tired she went upstairs to the bedroom, where she found seven little beds all in a row. She laid across three of them and fell fast asleep.

And that is how the dwarfs found her when they returned late that night. They agreed not to wake her, but let her sleep until morning.

The seven dwarfs had so many questions to ask Snow White. She told them about the wicked Queen and how she had tried to kill her. "Stay with us," begged the dwarfs. "The Queen will never find you here, for our house is deep in the forest."

So Snow White stayed. She cooked and cleaned and kept the tiny house tidy. And she promised the seven little men that she would never open the door to anyone when they were at work.

Meanwhile, back at the palace, the evil Queen stood in front of her magic mirror again. ''Magic Mirror on the wall, who is the fairest one of all?'' And the mirror answered, ''Snow White is the fairest of them all!''

The Queen almost smashed the mirror in her rage. ''Where is Snow White?'' she screamed. And the mirror replied, ''At the cottage of the seven dwarfs deep in the forest.''

Quickly the wicked Queen disguised herself as an old woman. Next she filled a big basket full of apples. Then she chose the biggest, rosiest apple — and with the help of magic spells and potions — made the apple poisonous.

Feeling very pleased with herself she set off for the home of the seven dwarfs.

"How very lucky!" sniggered the Queen. For there was Snow White drawing water from the well outside the little house.

The old woman startled Snow White, and she fled inside and bolted the door. "Don't be afraid of an old woman," cried the wicked Queen. "All I ask is a drink of water from your well, and I will give you my rosiest apple in return."

Snow White foolishly opened the window and held out her hand. The wicked Queen smiled. As soon as Snow White took one bite of the poisoned apple — she fell to the ground dead!

No sooner had the Queen returned to the Palace, than she pulled off her disguise and stood in front of her magic mirror. "You are the fairest of them all," the mirror told her. "Then Snow White is dead at last," smiled the Queen.

When the dwarfs returned from work, they guessed what had happened. Weeping with sorrow, they built a glass coffin for their beloved Snow White. They placed it in a forest clearing and watched over her day and night.

One day a Prince was riding through the forest.
When he saw the dwarfs looking so sad, he got off his
horse to see what was the matter.

He listened to their sad tale, and as he gazed down
at Snow White he fell in love with her at once.

As he bent down to kiss her, she opened her eyes
and sat up. The spell was broken. The Prince helped
her out of the glass coffin and all the dwarfs ran to hug
her.

The Prince asked Snow White to marry him and she gladly agreed.

The next time the wicked Queen stood in front of her Magic Mirror, it said to her, ''Snow White is the fairest of them all!'' That made her fall into such a jealous rage, that she fell down dead.

So the story ends happily after all, for the Prince, Snow White and the seven dwarfs — but not for the wicked Queen of course!

Lavender's blue, dilly, dilly,
Lavender's green,
When I am king, dilly, dilly,
You shall be queen.

Jack Sprat could eat no fat,
His wife could eat no lean,
And so between them both, you see,
They licked the platter clean.

Six little mice sat down to spin;
Pussy passed by and she peeped in.
What are you doing, my little men?
Weaving coats for gentlemen.
Shall I come in and cut off your threads?
No, no, Mistress Pussy, you'd bite off our heads.
Oh, no, I'll not; I'll help you to spin.
That may be so, but you don't come in.

Cock a doodle doo!
My dame has lost her shoe,
My master's lost his fiddling stick
And knows not what to do.

Cock a doodle doo!
What is my dame to do?
Till master finds his fiddling stick
She'll dance without her shoe.

Tom, Tom, the piper's son,
Stole a pig and away did run;
  The pig was eat,
  And Tom was beat,
And Tom went howling
  Down the street.

Roses are red,
  Violets are blue,

Sugar is sweet
  And so are you.

There was an old woman
Lived under a hill,
And if she's not gone
She lives there still.

Punch and Judy
Fought for a pie;
Punch gave Judy
A knock in the eye.

Says Punch to Judy,
'Will you have any more?'
Says Judy to Punch,
'My eye is too sore.'

Hickety, pickety, my black hen,
She lays eggs for gentlemen;
Sometimes nine, and sometimes ten,
Hickety, pickety, my black hen.

The north wind doth blow,
And we shall have snow,
And what will poor Robin do then,
Poor thing?
He'll sit in a barn,
And keep himself warm,
And hide his head under his wing,
Poor thing.

Monday

Tuesday

Wednesday

Monday's child is fair of face,
Tuesday's child is full of grace,
Wednesday's child is full of woe,
Thursday's child has far to go,
Friday's child is loving and giving,
Saturday's child works hard for its living,
And the child that's born on the Sabbath day
Is bonny and blithe, and good and gay.

Thursday

Friday

Saturday

Sunday

Little Tommy Tucker
    Sings for his supper,
What shall we give him?
    White bread and butter.
How shall he cut it
    Without e'er a knife?
How shall he marry
    Without e'er a wife?

Lucy Locket lost her pocket,
    Kitty Fisher found it;
Not a penny was there in it,
    Only ribbon round it.

The Lion and the Unicorn
    were fighting for the crown,
The Lion beat the Unicorn
    all round the town.
Some gave them white bread
    and some gave them brown,
And some gave them plum cake,
    and drummed them out of town.

Red sky at night,
Shepherd's delight;
Red sky in the morning,
Shepherd's warning.

PINOCCHIO

This story took place when all toys were made of
wood, and this tale is one of the strangest ever told.
Can you believe that an ordinary log of wood could
become a real live boy? Read on and you will see.

One day a carpenter picked
up a log of wood from a pile in
the corner of his workshop. He
was just about to chop it with
his axe when he heard a little
voice cry, "Don't hurt me!"
The voice came from the log of
wood.

The carpenter was so
terrified that he opened the door
and was about to throw the log
away, when who should come
by but Geppetto the toymaker.
"Just what I need," cried the
old man. "I am going to carve a
puppet that will behave just like
a real boy."

The carpenter was pleased to get rid of the talking log, because he thought it was bewitched!

Back at his toy shop Geppetto started work straight away. First he carved the puppet's head, and an amazing thing happened . . . the eyes blinked and the mouth smiled. Next he carved the body right down to the toes.

All of a sudden the puppet's foot flew up and kicked the old man on the nose. Instead of being angry, Geppetto was delighted with his talking puppet. "I shall call you Pinocchio," he smiled, "and you shall call me Father."

Geppetto began to teach Pinocchio how to walk. No sooner had the puppet learned, than he dashed out of the door and ran off down the street. Suddenly, a large policeman stepped out in front of Pinocchio and grabbed him.

By now a crowd had gathered and Geppetto was shouting at Pinocchio for running away. The angry crowd told the policeman to lock the old man up, for he was being cruel to the puppet.

So the policeman took poor Geppetto away to prison and Pinocchio ran off home.

You will have guessed by now that Pinocchio had a mind of his own, and was going to do exactly as he liked!

Later on Geppetto was let out of prison, because he had done nothing wrong. He made Pinocchio promise that he would go to school and learn to read.

That night Geppetto made him some new clothes. ''All I need now, father, is a spelling book,'' said Pinocchio. ''Then I shall be like other boys.''

At once the kind old man went out into the cold night and sold his only coat, to buy the spelling book.

Next morning, Pinocchio set off to school. But what was that wonderful sound he could hear? It was the music of a fairground.

He forgot all about school when he spotted a "Puppet Theatre". Without a second thought Pinocchio sold his spelling book to buy a ticket to go inside.

But when the puppets saw Pinocchio, they shouted for him to come up on stage to join them. The whole performance was ruined! The puppet-master threatened to throw Pinocchio on the fire — like a log of wood.

However, Pinocchio cried so pitifully that the puppet-master gave him five pieces of gold to take to Geppetto.

On his way home, Pinocchio met a sly fox and a cat who pretended to be blind. They told the puppet that if he buried his gold in a certain field — a miracle would happen. A tree would grow ladened with gold pieces.

It was a trick, of course! And when Pinocchio returned the next day the five gold pieces had gone, and so had the fox and the cat.

Not content with stealing his money, the fox and cat disguised themselves as robbers. They grabbed Pinocchio and tried to hang him from a tree, then ran off leaving him to die.

Luckily for Pinocchio, the Blue Fairy lived nearby and she saved him. She sent her poodle-dog footman to fetch the doctors . . . and what strange doctors they turned out to be . . . a crow, an owl and a cricket.

They all decided that Pinocchio was not dead after all — he was just a wicked puppet that had run away.

The Blue Fairy asked Pinocchio to tell her about his adventures, but the puppet would not tell the truth. The more he lied, the longer his nose grew. It grew so long it stuck out of the window.

The Blue Fairy clapped her hands and several birds flew down and they pecked at Pinocchio's nose until it was the right size once more.

''That's what comes of telling lies!'' laughed the Blue Fairy.

"How can I become a real boy?" Pinocchio asked the Blue Fairy.

"If you are good and go to school, you will have your dearest wish," she promised.

So Pinocchio went back to school. He worked hard, but unfortunately he soon grew tired of being good. He made friends with the naughtiest boy in the class.

One night they decided to run away to Toyland (where there is no school). They climbed into a special coach pulled by donkeys, and off they went.

It seemed fun at first, no lessons or work for months. Pinocchio and his friend loved it.

Then, without any warning, Pinocchio woke up to find he had grown a pair of donkey's ears. His friend had already changed into a donkey. All the children who came to Toyland were changed into donkeys, too, then sold.

A circus ringmaster bought poor Pinocchio and worked him very hard. One day, when he was jumping through a hoop, he hurt his leg.

The circus didn't want a lame donkey, so Pinocchio was sold again. This time to a man who wanted to make the donkey's skin into a drum.

He dragged Pinocchio into the sea to drown him, but the puppet slipped out of the skin and swam away laughing.

Suddenly a great shark rose up from the waves. Its monstrous jaws opened up wide and swallowed Pinocchio in one bite.

Down and down went the puppet — right to the
bottom of the shark's stomach. He felt very
frightened, until he heard a voice he knew.

There was old Geppetto sitting in a boat, carving
toys from the fish bone lying around.

Geppetto explained that he had gone to sea to look
for Pinocchio and had been swallowed by the shark.
He had lived on the food he had packed in his boat.

With the help of the Blue Fairy, the two sailed out of the shark's mouth and arrived safely back home.

Pinocchio sat down with Geppetto and told him all his adventures. He promised never to leave the old man again. And this time he kept his promise.

During the night, when Pinocchio was asleep, the Blue Fairy came by and granted Pinocchio his wish.

When he woke the next morning, he had become a real boy at last!

Old Mother Hubbard
    Went to her cupboard,
To fetch her poor dog a bone;
    But when she got there
The cupboard was bare
    And so the poor dog had none.

She went to the baker's
    To buy him some bread;
But when she came back
    The poor dog was dead.

She went to the joiner's
    To buy him a coffin.
But when she came back
    The poor dog was laughing.

She took a clean dish
    To get him some tripe;
But when she came back
    He was smoking a pipe.

She went to the fishmonger's
  To buy him some fish;
But when she came back
  He was licking the dish.

She went to the tavern
  For white wine and red;
But when she came back
  The dog stood on his head.

She went to the fruiterer's
  To buy him some fruit;
But when she came back
  He was playing the flute.

She went to the tailor's
  To buy him a coat;
But when she came back
  He was riding a goat.

She went to the hatter's
  To buy him a hat;
But when she came back
  He was feeding the cat.

She went to the barber's
     To buy him a wig;
But when she came back
     He was dancing a jig.

She went to the cobbler's
     To buy him some shoes;
But when she came back
     He was reading the news.

She went to the seamstress
     To buy him some linen;
But when she came back
     The dog was a-spinning.

She went to the hosier's
     To buy him some hose;
But when she came back
     He was dressed in his clothes.

The dame made a curtsey,
     The dog made a bow;
The dame said, 'Your servant,'
     The dog said, 'Bow-wow.'

Two little dicky birds
Sat upon a wall,

One called Peter,
One called Paul.

Fly away Peter,
Fly away Paul;

Come back Peter,
Come back Paul.

Peter Piper picked a peck
of pickled pepper;
A peck of pickled pepper
Peter Piper picked.
If Peter Piper picked a peck
of pickled pepper,
Where's the peck of pickled pepper
Peter Piper picked?

Here we go round the mulberry bush,
The mulberry bush, the mulberry bush,
Here we go round the mulberry bush,
On a cold and frosty morning.

Little Miss Muffet
Sat on a tuffet,
Eating her curds and whey;
There came a big spider,
Who sat down beside her
And frightened Miss Muffet away.

I see the moon,
  And the moon sees me;
God bless the moon,
  And God bless me.

See-saw, Margery Daw,
Johnny shall have a new master;
He shall have but a penny a day,
Because he can't work any faster.

Ding, dong, bell,
Pussy's in the well.
Who put her in?
Little Johnny Green.

Who pulled her out?
Little Tommy Stout.
What a naughty boy was that
To try to drown poor pussy cat,
Who never did him any harm,
But killed the mice in his father's barn.

The ThreeBears

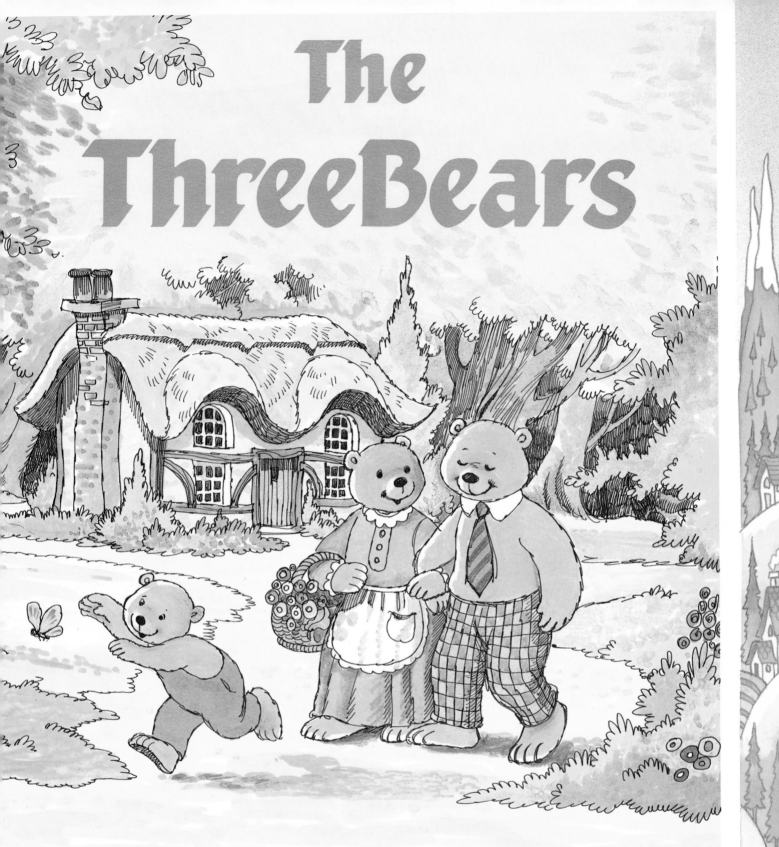

Once upon a time in a cottage deep in the woods,
lived three bears. There was Father Bear, Mother
Bear and a tiny little Baby Bear.

The Bear family lived very happily inside the
cottage. Each bear had its own bed, its own chair and
its own bowl.

Every morning Mother Bear got up early. She made a big saucepan full of porridge on the kitchen stove. When it was cooked, she poured the porridge into three bowls and put them on the kitchen table.

There was a great big bowl for Father Bear, a middle-sized bowl for Mother Bear and a tiny bowl for Baby Bear.

First Father Bear took a big mouthful. "My porridge is too hot," he yelled in a great loud voice.

Then Mother Bear tasted a spoonful. "Oh dear!" she gasped. "This porridge is very hot indeed."

Then last of all Baby Bear sat down in front of his tiny bowl. "My porridge is too hot as well," cried Baby Bear in his squeaky voice. And he began to cry.

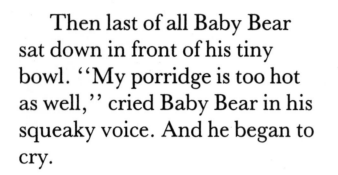

It was such a lovely morning, they all decided to go for a walk in the woods until their porridge cooled.

No sooner had they left the cottage than a little girl came skipping along the path. Her

name was Goldilocks, because she had lots of golden curls. All of a sudden, through a clearing in the trees, she spied the bears' cottage.

"I wonder who lives in here?" she cried. "I think I'll take a look inside."

She peeped in the door and saw three bowls of porridge on the table, just ready to eat.

Goldilocks was so hungry she decided to try some. The first was too hot, the second too sweet, but the third little bowl was just right. Goldilocks gobbled the lot.

"That porridge was lovely,"
said Goldilocks, "I think I'll
take a look around." So she
tiptoed into the next room.
First she found Father
Bear's great big chair — but it
was too high for her to reach.

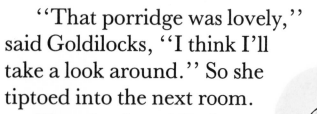

Next she found Mother
Bear's middle-sized chair —
but it was too soft to sit in.

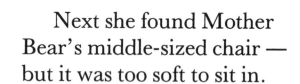

Then she spotted Baby Bear's tiny chair. So she sat
down. Suddenly, there was a loud CRACK, and the
chair broke. Poor Goldilocks fell with a thump onto
the floor.

Now Goldilocks was feeling rather sleepy, so she crept upstairs to have a little rest. First she saw Father Bear's great big bed. Goldilocks climbed up, but it was so hard and uncomfortable she soon jumped off.

Next she tried Mother Bear's middle-sized bed, but it was so soft Goldilocks sank right down into the covers. Quickly she scrambled out again.

At last she found Baby Bear's little tiny bed. It looked so comfortable, she pulled back the covers and jumped in. Very soon she was fast asleep.

But who's this walking along the path up to the cottage door? It's the three bears back from their morning walk . . . feeling very hungry!

When Father Bear saw his great big bowl, he began to shout, "Somebody has been eating my porridge!"

When Mother Bear saw her middle-sized bowl, she said in a cross voice, "Somebody has been eating my porridge!"

When Baby Bear saw his empty bowl he cried, "Somebody has been eating my porridge and has eaten it all up!"

Then Father Bear said,
"Somebody has been sitting in
my chair."
    And Mother Bear said,
"Somebody has been sitting in
my chair as well."

    Poor Baby Bear cried, "Somebody has been sitting
in my chair and has broken it in bits."

The three bears rushed upstairs to see what they could find.

"Somebody has been sleeping in my bed," Father Bear growled.

"And somebody has been sleeping in my bed, too," Mother Bear cried.

"Somebody has been sleeping in my bed,"
shouted Baby Bear, "and here she is!"

All this shouting woke poor Goldilocks up. What a
shock she got when she saw the three bears peering
down at her.

Goldilocks jumped out of bed, ran down the stairs and out of the cottage as fast as she could. She ran down the path and all the way home. And to this day, Goldilocks has never gone walking in the woods alone.

Jack and Jill
Went up the hill,
To fetch a pail of water;

Jack fell down,
And broke his crown,
And Jill came tumbling after.

Doctor Foster went to Gloucester
　　In a shower of rain;
He stepped in a puddle,
　　Right up to his middle,
And never went there again.

Girls and boys come out to play,
The moon doth shine as bright as day.
Leave your supper and leave your sleep,
And come with your playfellows into the street.
Come with a whoop and come with a call,
Come with a good will or not at all.
Up the ladder and down the wall,
A half-penny loaf will serve us all;
You find milk, and I'll find flour,
And we'll have a pudding in half an hour.

The Man in the Moon
Looked out of the moon,
Looked out of the moon and said,
"'Tis time for all children on the earth
To think about getting to bed!"

I love little pussy,
    Her coat is so warm,
And if I don't hurt her,
    She'll do me no harm.
So I'll not pull her tail,
    Or drive her away,
But Pussy and I
    Very gently will play.
She will sit by my side,
    And I'll give her some food,
And she'll like me because
    I am gentle and good.

Fee, fi, fo, fum,
I smell the blood of an Englishman:
Be he alive or be he dead,
I'll grind his bones to make my bread.

Here am I,
little Jumping Joan,
When I'm by myself,
I'm all alone.

Hark, hark, the dogs do bark,
   The beggars are coming to town;
Some in rags and some in jags,
   And one in a velvet gown.

Ring-a-ring o'roses,
A pocket full of posies,
 A-tishoo! A-tishoo!
We all fall down.

Charley Parley stole the barley
Out of the baker's shop.
The baker came out,
and gave him a clout,
Which made poor Charley hop.

There was an old woman who lived in a shoe;
She had so many children she didn't know what to do.
She gave them some broth without any bread;
Then whipped them all soundly and put them to bed.

Rock-a-bye, baby, on the tree-top.
When the wind blows
The cradle will rock;

When the bough breaks,
The cradle will fall,
Down will come baby,
Cradle and all.

Heeper-peeper, chimney sweeper,
　　Had a wife and couldn't keep her.
Had another, didn't love her,
　　Up the chimney he did shove her.

Please to remember
The fifth of November,
Gunpowder treason and plot;
I see no reason
Why gunpowder treason
Should ever be forgot.

Penny for the guy

BEAUTY AND THE BEAST

Once upon a time there lived a very rich merchant. He owned a splendid house and beautiful gardens. He had three ships which sailed to many countries and brought back lots of treasure.

The merchant had four sons and three daughters. The youngest was so lovely that everyone called her Beauty. The two elder daughters were lazy and bad-tempered, but Beauty was both kind and gentle.

One dreadful day a messenger arrived with very bad news. One of the merchant's ships had sunk, another had been attacked by pirates and the third was lost at sea.

The merchant was ruined, overnight he became a poor man. His two elder daughters stamped and screamed because they could have no more jewels or fine clothes.

However, the youngest daughter, Beauty, comforted her father. "I love you more than money or clothes," she said kindly. "Be happy! We still have each other."

Because they were now so poor, they had to move out of their splendid house and live in a tiny cottage. The sisters hated their plain clothes and humble home.

On the other hand, Beauty was never more happy. She cooked and cleaned from morning 'til night and took care of the whole family.

One day another messenger came to see the merchant. This time he brought good news. The ship everyone thought was lost, had returned full of treasure.

The merchant set out at once to bring back his fortune. But before he left he asked each of his daughters what special gift they would like him to bring back.

"As many jewels as you can find," snapped one.

"As many clothes as you can carry," sneered the other.

Beauty just smiled. "In my garden there are no flowers, only vegetables, so I would like a single red rose!"

When he came to the end of his long journey, the merchant was in for a great shock. Thieves had boarded his ship during the night and stolen all his treasure. Feeling very tired and down-hearted, the poor merchant set off for home.

For many hours along the road, his head hung down in despair. Something made him look up — there in the distance he could see a magnificent house. The merchant felt he had to take a closer look. And there growing in the middle of the garden was a beautiful red rose. ''I must take it home for Beauty,'' said the merchant and he reached out and picked the flower.

At once the garden was filled with a terrifying sound, like the roar of an angry lion. The merchant fell on his knees in fear.

There in front of him stood a terrible beast. He had the face of a lion and the body of a man, his teeth were sharp and his claws long.

"It is death to steal my roses!" snarled the Beast. How the merchant begged the Beast to spare his life. Quickly he told the Beast all about his misfortunes, and his promise to bring Beauty back a single red rose.

"Merchant," growled the Beast. "I will spare your life on one condition. Bring one of your daughters back here to live with me — or you will die!"

The merchant was too afraid to say no so he gave his word and turned away sadly.

When he reached home, his family were overjoyed to see him, until he told them of his promise to the Beast. Then their joy soon turned to sorrow.

"You can go!" the two sisters shrieked, pointing at Beauty. "You asked for the stupid red rose — not us!" Straight away kind Beauty said: "I will go back with you father, I'm sure the Beast means no harm."

Feeling very unhappy, Beauty and her father said
farewell and set off on their journey. Strange to say,
the nearer they came to the Beast's home — the more
beautiful the scenery became.

At last they arrived and passed through the gates
into the garden. Beauty had never seen anything so
lovely. Flowers bloomed and butterflies danced and
peacocks strutted on the lawns. In front of the
fountains a table was set full of food, in case they felt
hungry after their journey.

As soon as they had eaten, without any warning, the Beast appeared! He came towards Beauty, his great shaggy head bowed low. Beauty was really afraid, but she tried not to show it.

Soon it was time for her father to return home, and Beauty was left alone with the Beast.

Inside the great house, Beauty was given her own room with everything she could ever want to make her happy. The Beast had done his best to make her feel welcome.

On the table in her room the Beast had left her a magic mirror. Whenever Beauty looked into it, she could see her home, her father and brothers and even her bad-tempered sisters.

The Beast was so kind to her, that Beauty became very fond of him.

One day, as she gazed into the magic mirror, she saw her father lying on his bed looking very ill.

She found the Beast at once and begged him to let her return home. He loved her so much that he agreed. "Return in three months or I might die," he told her. Then he gave Beauty a ring. "Put it on when you wish to return to me."

So Beauty set off for home, feeling sad to leave the Beast as well as longing to see her father.
Although the merchant was very ill, he felt much better when he saw his daughter safe and well.

So happy was Beauty at home with her family, that three months soon slipped by.

One morning, Beauty happened to glance into her magic mirror, and there was the Beast looking very ill indeed. "I must return at once," cried Beauty, "or my poor Beast will die!" Quickly she found the ring the Beast had given her.

The moment she slipped it on her finger she found herself back in the Beast's home.

Beauty ran from room to room searching for the Beast, but the house was empty. She searched everywhere in the gardens and called his name, but there was no answer.

Last of all she went to the place she loved the best — the rose garden. There lay the Beast stretched out on the grass.

"I should have come back sooner," Beauty sobbed. "I'm afraid my poor Beast is dead."

She knelt beside him and hugged him. "Don't die, dear Beast!" she begged. "You have been so kind to me that I have grown to love you."

As she spoke these words, lightning lit up the sky and the Beast became a handsome Prince.

"You have broken the spell cast on me by a wicked witch," cried the Prince. "At last I am free to ask you to marry me."

In a little while Beauty did marry the Prince and they were very happy together.

The Prince asked Beauty's father and brothers to come and live with them, but not the bad tempered sisters!

Some times Beauty and the Prince got out the magic mirror to look at them both in their cottage, still arguing and fighting with each other. And I expect they always will!